Contents

Rigby is an imprint of Pearson Education Limited, a company incorporated in England and Wales, having its registered office at Edinburgh Gate, Harlow, Essex, CM20 2JE. Registered company number: 872828

www.rigbyed.co.uk

Help and support for teachers, plus the widest range of education solutions

Rigby is a registered trademark of Reed Elsevier Inc, Licensed to Pearson Education Limited

Head to Head first published 2004

'Heads or Tails' © Kathryn White 2004
'Girls Watch' © Kathryn White 2004
'School Fête Shoot-out' © Harcourt Education Limited 2004

Series editor: Shirley Bickler

08

10 9 8 7 6 5

Head to Head
ISBN 9780433035411

Group reading pack with teaching notes
ISBN 9780433035718

Illustrated by Sholto Walker, Sharon Harmer and Annie Boberg

Cover illustration © Richard Johnson

Designed by StoreyBooks

Repro by Digital Imaging, Glasgow

Printed and bound in China by CTPS

Heads or Tails

written by Kathryn White

illustrated by Sholto Walker

This story takes place in a coffee-growing, mountain village in Jamaica.

"You two fighting again?" Miss Mace bellowed across the yard. A crowd of children scattered, like frightened deer.

Miss Mace swept up to the two bruised boys. Her red blouse flapped in the hot winds like a bullfighter's cape and her grey cotton skirt flew around her striding legs. She yanked Leroy and Joshua back onto their dusty feet. Her beaded bangles jingled in their ears as she frogmarched them to the schoolhouse.

"Sit," Miss Mace ordered. "You two have done my patience to the quick."

Leroy and Joshua sat as stiff as statues, as far from each other as possible, facing the mighty Miss Mace.

"One whole month you've been making our lives miserable," she snapped.

Leroy and Joshua frowned.

"If you two don't want to make up, that's fine by me, but scrapping, kicking and hollering like wild hyenas isn't. You want to behave like animals then…"

A smile grew across Miss Mace's face as if a button had just clicked in her head. The boys sensed something brewing.

Miss Mace continued, "If you want to behave like animals then you'll be an animal in the school play. One that fits your characters."

"I'm going to be the hero, Anancy," Leroy thought with delight.

As everyone else filed into class, Joshua was thinking exactly the same thing.

Once class was seated, Miss Mace made her announcement. "August 6th is Independence Day, when all of Jamaica celebrates with plays and songs, so, I want our smartest child to play our folk hero Anancy…"

Everyone held their breath.

"Victoria," announced Miss Mace.

All the boys looked stunned. The girls cheered triumphantly and patted Victoria on the back.

"There's going to be more smart roles to fill, but," continued Miss Mace with a broad grin, "Joshua will be the mule."

Guffaws of laughter rang out. Joshua looked at Miss Mace in disbelief. "But, miss…I can't act," he protested.

"Joshua boy, you don't need to act, you just be yourself," Miss Mace replied sharply.

There was another great wave of laughter. Joshua's face fell.

Leroy laughed louder than everyone until Miss Mace flashed him a dark look. "Leroy, why are you laughing?" she said.

Leroy's grin froze on his face.

"You're going to be the mule too," she said.

Leroy gulped.

"It's just a matter of which end, the front or the rear," she said.

Now the class was in uproar as everyone
stamped their feet. Miss Mace banged her desk to
silence the class. "Friendship is about forgiveness
and compromise," she said. "COMPROMISE!" she
repeated, staring at Leroy and Joshua. "Whoever
spells the word correctly can choose… head
or tail!"

Miss Mace signalled. Leroy stood up like a condemned man and walked slowly to the board. His hand wavered, then he wrote 'COMPRUMEYES'.

The air in the room was as thick as treacle. "Sit!" said Miss Mace.

Joshua snatched the marker from Leroy's hand, stormed to the board and scribbled 'COMPRUMISE'.

"My! You're both wrong," exclaimed Miss Mace with false surprise. "Still, as Joshua's only one letter out," Miss Mace scribbled 'COMPROMISE' on the board, "Joshua chooses."

Joshua sulked. "The head, miss."

Leroy's heart pounded. "You're for it now," he whispered angrily to Joshua.

"I'll watch my rear," Joshua sniggered.

Leroy's blood boiled.

Miss Mace declared, "Heads or tails, it makes no difference to me. You're both the mule."

After class Leroy and Joshua sped out of
school, but they were too slow. A crowd of
boys followed them through the village, taunting
and jeering, "Eeeyaaaw," and blowing
loud raspberries.

Leroy felt humiliated. "This is your fault," he
hissed at Joshua.

"Yeah?" Joshua said, almost in tears. "Who
started it, donkey?"

Desperate, Leroy ran off.

"Auntie, I've got gripes," Leroy said weakly to Aunt Jessie the following day.

"Two fried eggs and sweet bread sure don't seem like gripes to me. School!" Aunt Jessie said, jostling Leroy out.

Leroy had other ideas. He hurried off as if he was going to school, then ducked behind a tree. Then Leroy jumped over Mr Parker's rickety fence, sneaked into his own yard and wriggled back into his house through Aunt Jessie's bedroom window. He landed softly on his hands. He heard Aunt Jessie humming in the kitchen.

Leroy opened the wardrobe door and hid in the darkness. He fell asleep and awoke to the smell of Aunt Jessie's roasted coffee. Leroy's tummy rumbled as the clock ticked away the long afternoon, until at long last he heard shouts from the children returning from school.

11

Leroy climbed out of the window, crept around the side of his house and, whistling a tune, marched in the front door.

Aunt Jessie was stirring rice. "You're gonna be hungry after all that school stuff," Aunt Jessie smiled, handing Leroy his dinner.

"Sure am," Leroy said uneasily.

Early next morning Leroy was off again, sneaking over fences and through windows, and hiding in the wardrobe all day. "Miss Mace must have someone else for the mule by now," he thought.

On the third day, as Leroy lay in the wardrobe, he heard a voice that made him quiver. "Leroy! Out of my wardrobe now."

Leroy slowly opened the door. His brown eyes grew wide in horror. Aunt Jessie was standing firmly beside Miss Mace.

"What have you got to say for yourself?" Miss Mace said, folding her arms into an angry cradle.

"I was looking for something," Leroy muttered.

"Oh, my!" Miss Mace rolled her eyes in disbelief. "Leroy has been away from school, looking for something in the wardrobe for three days. Have you found it yet?"

The two fierce women towered over Leroy like the Blue Mountains. He was speechless.

13

"Here," said Aunt Jessie, "I've found what you've been looking for." She thrust the mule costume at Leroy. The mule's tail swung from side to side, like a snake on a branch.

Leroy recoiled in horror. It reminded him of the dead animal Mrs Tibbits wore around her neck to church each Sunday. Aunt Jessie said Mrs Tibbits wore it for luck. Leroy thought it was the unluckiest animal he'd ever seen.

14

Leroy's eyes followed the tail, rocking on the end of Aunt Jessie's slim fingers.

"Wear it," Aunt Jessie commanded. "It might get rid of that stubborn streak you've been wearing all month."

"Uh huh, that's true, Aunt Jessie," Miss Mace said, nodding fiercely in agreement. Leroy reluctantly took the costume.

"You'll make a good mule, Leroy," said Aunt Jessie, grinning.

"Come to the schoolhouse in half an hour. You're going to practise being a mule's behind," said Miss Mace.

"But what about the mule's head?" Leroy blurted hopefully.

"It'll be there," Miss Mace said firmly. "Just like you."

She swung round, her dress billowing out like an orange tent, and marched out of the room with Aunt Jessie striding behind.

Leroy fell onto the bed and groaned. All was lost. He was the mule's rear end. He'd longed to be Anancy; to perform daring feats to an amazed audience.

Leroy looked darkly at the photograph of his mother on the sideboard. She sure was pretty, but that was a long time ago. He wondered what she was like now. Aunt Jessie said maybe one day his mum would come back for him. She had been too young to have a child and cope with all that wailing and washing, so she had given Leroy to Aunt Jessie.

Leroy's heart sank. He reckoned if his mum was home she'd have said, "My Leroy's not going to be the mule's behind. He's too clever for that." Aunt Jessie sure was a hard woman.

Waiting at school, Joshua sat shamefaced on the stage, fiddling with the mule's head.

Leroy plodded in and put on his tail. "Right! Play's on tomorrow, ready or not," Miss Mace said, and rehearsals began.

It was painfully hot in the mule suit. "Not that way," Miss Mace shouted desperately. "This way."

"Miss, I can't see where I'm going," Leroy pleaded.

"You need trust, boy. Just follow the head and don't complain."

Leroy was suffocating and kept tripping over his loose trainer laces. By 9 o'clock Miss Mace called, "Stop, you'll do. Least you can't be trouble in a mule suit."

The boys stepped out of the hall gasping for cool air.

"Painful, man," said Joshua grimly.

"Sure was," Leroy said glumly.

"I skived too," Joshua confessed, grinning. "I hid in the loo."

Leroy beamed. "Looks like we're in it together."

Joshua put up his palm. "Hey! I've got an idea," he said. "Let's take this mule for a spin."

"Yeah," said Leroy. "Let's show 'em." They slapped palms.

The following
night the school hall
was packed. Mrs
Tibbits, wearing her
dead animal, sat
up front.

The play was going
well…until the mule
came on.

"Ready?" said Joshua.

"Ready!" Leroy replied.

Miss Mace scowled at the mule. It danced
to the left. Then hopped to the
right. It skipped to the
front and swirled to
the back.

19

Miss Mace reached for the tail to yank it offstage. But suddenly the audience began clapping a rhythm and the mule leapt and hopped in perfect timing.

Finally, it jumped onto the table and tapped to the audience chants. Everyone cheered with delight.

Miss Mace marched onto the stage. "We all want to thank Anancy," she said. Victoria bowed.

Then the rest of the troupe stepped up and waved.

"But," Miss Mace said with pride, "a special thank you to our clever mule because it compromised and danced an unforgettable dance."

Joshua pulled off the mule's head and stood beside Leroy.

"Cool," they said laughing, bowing proudly together.

Girls Watch

written by Kathryn White

illustrated by Sharon Harmer

Chapter 1

Josie peered through
the mesh fence.
There they stood,
towering like
monsters in the
dusky light. Half pipes,
boards and grinder bars
– new, exciting, waiting
for Josie to ride them to
their limits.

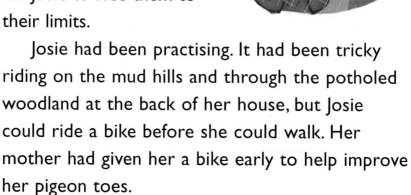

Josie had been practising. It had been tricky
riding on the mud hills and through the potholed
woodland at the back of her house, but Josie
could ride a bike before she could walk. Her
mother had given her a bike early to help improve
her pigeon toes.

Soon her mother regretted it. "Girl, so far you've broken both wrists and cracked a tooth. I reckon you were better off with pigeon toes."

But for Josie, riding her bike was what she did best and when she was happiest. Now, as if by magic, the new park was opening in time for her 12th birthday. She looked at the ramps, awestruck. "Wicked," she said to her best friend Lily.

"I'd rather have a water chute as high as Winberry Hill," Lily said wistfully. "Imagine, it would take five whole minutes to whizz down the slide, turning and twisting, spinning and then SPLASH! into a warm pool of water. Now that's wicked."

"What are *you* doing here?" said Mara acidly. Mara was standing behind Josie and Lily with her cronies around her like bees around honey. "You're keen. Boys don't arrive until the gates open tomorrow."

It puzzled Josie how such an in-your-face, notice-me-boys group of girls always appeared from nowhere. Lily reckoned they were aliens from another planet, hooked onto their mobile phones all day to receive intergalactic orders from the leaders of Planet Bimbo.

"What time does it open?" said Josie coolly.

"For us ...10. For you ... never," Mara said, flicking her beaded afro fringe. She was pretty and she knew it. The group sniggered.

Mara's family, like Josie's, came from Jamaica, but it didn't make her any friendlier towards Josie. Mara didn't like her. Josie never figured out why, though she guessed it was because she didn't copy Mara like her robot cronies.

Josie wore her hoody and skater jeans and kept her hair tied tightly back from her face. She felt hair was just a problem and that spending hours threading beads through each strand as Mara did was crazier and grosser than nit combing.

"Mara and the Clones," Lily whispered to Josie.

"What?" hissed Anna, one of the Clones.

"I said Mara's got a cool phone," Lily said dryly.

"I know," said Mara, flicking up the tiger print cover on the display. The keypad lit up. "Call me," she ordered Josie.

"When?" Josie was genuinely puzzled.

"Now...moron. Then everyone can hear my ringtone."

"Loser..." Lily coughed into her hands.

"I don't have a mobile," said Josie, bored.

Mara smirked, "No, you wouldn't." Her group giggled nervously.

"I'll call you, Mara," simpered Anna as she keyed a name into her phone. Within seconds, music rang out from Mara's mobile.

"Wow," said Anna, "that's number one in the charts."

"I know that, idiot," said Mara smugly.

Anna blushed.

"We've got our places marked," Mara said to Josie. She pointed to the top of the vert. "That's my patch. It's sorted with Mike and the boys. I don't want to find *you* there in the morning." She gave Josie a hard stare.

"We're not going to just sit and watch," said Josie mockingly.

"What else are you going to do? Make a video?" sniggered Mara.

"Leave her alone, she's going to ride her Huffy!" blurted Lily, wondering why the words had tumbled from her mouth.

Mara looked daggers
at Lily.

Lily and Josie glared
back. For a few long
moments, both sides
stared each other out until
Mara broke the tense
silence. She shoved past Lily
and stormed up to Josie.
"DON'T GET IN MY WAY."

Josie stood her ground, but
had no intention of getting into a
fight the night before the park opened. She'd
waited too long for this, there was too much
at stake.

"What is your problem, Mara?"

Mara stepped back, glowering. "Come on, you
lot, let's leave these saddos to dream on." She
marched her cronies away.

"Phew, Josie," said Lily. "I thought you were going to fight her."

"What, and ruin my best biking hand?" Josie said, shakily putting up her hand. "This is precious, Lil, I need it to do my greatest stunt yet."

"What's that?"

"Just wait and see," Josie said, her eyes lighting up. "Just you wait and see."

 **Chapter 2**

The gates opened and the new park burst into life.

There were shouts, whistles and cheers as everyone took to the ramps. Bladers shot around the outside track, some in pairs, others just cruising and listening to music.

On the half pipes, skateboard wheels glided the riders from one end, then, tilting, glided them lazily back to the other. Groups of kids sat scattered on the grass, some just spectators, others keen, hopeful learners.

Sitting, posing, centre-top of the vert, were Mara and her fans.

Josie and Lily walked the bike over. They watched Mike fly down the vert, do a wheelie and fly back up the other side.

Mara and the gang giggled and flirted.

Next was Sam, straight down the vert, up and turning just as his wheel came over the top of the platform. Mara's gang wolf-whistled admiringly towards Mike and the boys.

31

As each rider did his trick, the next stood around waiting for his turn. Josie joined the end of the line and slowly moved up. She looked over the top of the vert.

It was steep. Her heart was thumping.

Now it was her turn. Clutching the handlebars she stepped forward. Suddenly, a hand thrust across her path.

"Where do you think you're going?" Mike was staring darkly down at her.

"It's my go," said Josie, her heart pounding so hard she thought it would burst.

Mike sniggered, "GIRLS WATCH."

Josie shook with anger.

Mara's gang hollered and whistled from the opposite side of the vert. "Off the ramp, loser."

Josie's face grew hot with rage. "It's my go," she insisted, her voice quivering. A group had gathered around them.

"Tell you what," sneered Mike, "you go if…you can do this."

Mike leapt off the ramp, shot across the vert and landed his wheels dead centre on the opposite platform. He held the bike in a toothpick lock and then shot back to where Josie stood.

A cheer went up.

Josie stepped forward, trembling. She clutched her handlebars till her knuckles went white. Then she leapt.

She blasted down the ramp and sped up the other side. Controlled, she held her Huffy in the toothpick lock, jumped back and hit the platform inches away from Mike.

There was a stunned silence.

"Not bad…for a girl," said Mike. Then he shot down the vert, did a triple bar-spin and returned smirking. He bowed as cheers erupted.

Josie took a deep breath, then leapt off.

She did a pro-hop and kept descending down the ramp. At the other side she made a one-eighty and landed perfectly in an ice-pick lock, then finally she made an incredible three-sixty alley-oop!

"AWESOME!" shouted the crowds.

Mike was livid. Staring across the vert, he clenched his teeth and went for it.

Whizzing down, he shot up the ramp, thrust his front wheel onto the wall and came to a sudden, jarring halt. He veered sideways out of control. The bike flipped over and Mike tumbled, crashing down the vert.

"He's dead!" Mara screamed hysterically.

Mike gurgled from the wreckage, "I'm dying."

Sam slid down the vert to pull Mike from under the bike.

"NO!" Josie shouted. "Don't move him." She could see Mike's leg entangled in the bars.

"Aahhghh! Get an ambulance!" screeched Mike. "My leg's coming off."

Josie slid down and crouched next to him. "Don't be a nerd, Mike," she said calmly, resisting a desire to laugh. "You've just broken it."

"I'm gonna die," Mike whimpered.

"You'll be OK," Josie reassured him. "Nearly every time I do a new trick I break something. It drives Mum crazy."

Mike had begun to shiver so Josie took off her jacket and put it over him. She stayed next to him, talking quietly, until the paramedics arrived.

"Looks like we've got our first park casualty," the medic said with a knowing smile. "Leg's broken. Just as well your friend kept you still."

"Aren't I going to die?" groaned Mike.

The paramedic laughed. "Maybe when you're ninety!"

Chapter 3

Weeks later, Josie waited on the platform at the top of the vert. She watched Mike hop across the park on his crutches as he had done every day since the accident. He waved up at her and she smiled back.

Sam shot down the ramp, did a wobbly alley-oop and returned to Josie on the platform. "I still can't get that right," he said, frustrated.

"You're leaning too far forward," said Josie. "Do it like this." And she flew down the ramp and did a perfect alley-oop.

"AWESOME!" Mike called from below.

Josie grinned at him. "I'll show you how when the plaster comes off."

"Cool," said Mike.

All at once, Mara and her cronies appeared from the other side of the vert. Mara shouted up at Josie, "Still showing off?"

"Why don't you have a go, Mara?" Mike taunted. "Scared?"

Josie laughed. "Don't you know, Mike... GIRLS WATCH."

School Fête Shoot-out

written by Haydn Middleton

illustrated by Annie Boberg

Head to Head

School Fête Shoot-out!

Amazing Saturday Afternoon Showdown!

Alice Foster shoots against Matt Henderson

Four years ago, safety inspectors shut down the old swimming pool at Fleetwood Primary. To reopen it, the school had to make repairs that would cost £2000. So that's exactly how much the staff, pupils and parents aimed to raise at the summer fête.

When the fête ended, however, they were still some way short of their target – until one very quick-witted pupil stepped in…

* * *

Mr Pitt backed into the classroom carrying a huge pile of papers. "Right," he said, "I've marked your maths tests."

42

"Oh not *now*, sir," groaned Jay, who had answered only five questions and got at least three of those wrong. "You'll ruin our summer holidays!"

Ignoring him, Mr Pitt went around giving back the tests. He handed one to the cool-looking boy sitting next to Jay. "Congratulations, Matt," he said. "You scored eighty-nine per cent."

"Woo, woo, woo!" yelled every boy in the room. Matt raised his baseball cap and nodded to the left and right.

"However," Mr Pitt went on, "that was two per cent *less* than the mark scored by Alice..."

All the girls screamed as Alice held her test paper in the air, closed her eyes and purred, "Yesss!"

43

"Goodness," said Mr Pitt. "Why all the noise?"

"Oh you know how it is, sir!" cried Emma, hugging Alice proudly. "Matt's top boy at everything and Alice is always the best girl – but as we've just seen, GIRLS RULE!!!"

An enormous female cheer swept the room.

"We'll be back," muttered Jay. "Just wait till the disco tonight."

"Ah, Jay," said Mr Pitt, glancing with a sad smile at the next sheet before handing it back. "When are you *ever* going to put that brain of yours to work? You scored seven per cent."

HOT SUMMER NIGHT!

Years 5 and 6 End-of-Term Disco

7.00p.m – 10.00pm

Best Dancer Award to be judged by

Mystery International

Mega-Star Guest!!!

"You'll walk off with that prize," Jay yelled at Matt near the end of the disco. Matt's moves must surely have impressed the mystery judge. But Emma overheard what Jay said.

"In your dreams, Mr Seven Per Cent!" she laughed. "There's only one winner here tonight." She nodded across at Alice, who was dancing as if her life depended on it.

When the disco was over the Head took the DJ's mike. "School," she boomed, "let's hear it for one of the world's top recording artists... Miss Kylie Minogue!"

The gasps and shrieks turned into boos as Mrs Chen appeared, wearing a vast polystyrene Kylie head. More gasps, shrieks and boos filled the hall when she announced the winner of the Best Dancer Award.

"That's *so* unfair!" fumed Alice to her shell-shocked crew. "But term's not over for another week yet. I'll get even!"

Next morning, Mr Pitt took a long hard look at the class after registration. "You boys and girls have become so terribly competitive," he said. "This does concern me. Has it never crossed your minds to co-operate?"

"Oh we do co-operate, sir," said Jay with a hurt look. "We boys co-operate all the time...so we can whup the girls!"

"Could you *be* more immature?" Emma asked as the boys hi-fived him.

"Well, here's something even you can't be competitive about," said Mr Pitt, passing out a letter for everyone to take home. "It's about the summer fête next Saturday afternoon."

Dear Parents, Guardians and Children

This year, by popular demand, all the funds raised at the fête will go towards restoring the old school swimming pool. We need to raise £2000 before work can begin during the summer break. At present we are still looking for people to run the following stalls: coconut shy, wet-sponge throwing, pillow fight. All offers of help gratefully received.

Jay glanced at Matt, then glanced at Alice – and deep in his under-worked brain a plan began to form.

That night Jay contacted Matt on the Internet:

Jay: Just heard – Alice is running wet-sponge stall. You've got the coconut shy next to it, right?

Matt: Yeah? Why?

Jay: So you can *whup* her, top boy! Make more cash. Show her who's the fund-raising boss!

Matt: Yeah?

Jay: YEAH! Just watch. I'll help you make £100 at least! You'll be a fête fund-raising god!

At the same time, Emma was texting Alice:

51

The school really couldn't have picked a worse day for the fête. Not only would there be a street party just around the corner. There was also a World Cup football match live on TV *and* a free pop festival in the park.

"It's too late to change the date," the Head announced at assembly. "Anyway, let's look on the bright side: not *everyone* likes parties or football or pop music!"

Every pupil's jaw dropped. Nobody could think of a single person who didn't like one of those things. It looked as if the swimming pool would have to stay shut – but Jay was still planning...

Two days before the fête, he stopped Mrs Chen in the corridor. "Please, miss, could you count up Matt and Alice's takings the minute the fête is over?"

"I might be able to. Why's that?"

"So you can present *this* to whoever's raised the most cash." He produced a home-made cardboard crown. On the front he had printed FTF.

"What does that stand for?"

"Fête's Top Fund-raiser!"

So competitive! This really does concern me.

At least he's taking an interest in the fête, and we need all the interest we can get.

Local TV weathergirl Maggie Manning opened the fête. Quite a few people turned up to get her autograph, then most of them stayed to have a go on the stalls. The Head crossed her fingers. "Not a bad start," she kept saying.

"Alice's queue is longer than ours," Jay soon pointed out to Matt. (Cleverly she had put the grumpy school caretaker in the hot-seat. Everyone wanted to throw wet sponges at *him* – including the teachers.) "We need to attract more punters," said Jay, disappearing into the school.

He came back with a square of white card nailed to a pole.

MATT'S COCONUT SHY SERIOUSLY SPECIAL OFFER!!

TWO GOES FOR THE PRICE OF THREE!!!

"An offer they can't refuse! I'll walk around the field with it," said Jay.

"Er… shouldn't that be three for the price of two?" asked Matt.

"Doh!" said Jay. "*I* know that. *You* know that. But do *they* know it?" And ten minutes later half a dozen parents with more money than sense had taken him up on his 'offer'!

Matt and Alice were doing much better business than anyone else. Mainly boys flocked to Matt's stall, mainly girls to Alice's.

"Matt for Top Fund-raiser!" yelled the boys with every throw at the coconuts.

"We want Alice!" cried the girls with each hurled sponge.

But at around 4 o'clock everything went wrong. That was when the World Cup match kicked off, a band came on stage in the park, and the street party barbecue began.

The size of the crowd halved. Then it halved again, and again. There was no chance now of raising £2000.

"Bye-bye swimming pool," sighed Emma.

It was like a ghost fête now, the thud-thud-thudding music from the park crushing everyone's spirits even more.

Mrs Chen had plenty of time to count up the takings *before* close-down at 5 o'clock. The total was just £1620 – £380 short of the target. But who would be the FTF? Everyone left at the fête was still dead keen to know.

"You're not going to believe this," Mrs Chen told them, "but Matt and Alice have raised exactly the same amount: £88!" She held up Jay's crown. "So how do we decide who gets this?"

"Penalty shoot-out!" Jay piped up. He nodded at Mr Pitt who had been keeping goal – very badly – for Beat the Goalie.

"Good call!" cried Matt and Alice, both excellent footballers.

"But let them shoot against each other," Jay went on. "Five shots each and see who scores more. And they can't do it for free. How much are you charging for each shot, sir?"

"Twenty pence," said Mr Pitt.

"Okay, we'll double that. So someone's got to pay for ten shots at 40p a shot. That's £4. Who's going to be the lucky punter?"

Ten people rushed up offering coins.

"Goodness," gasped Mr Pitt. "I do believe Jay's finally got his brain working!"

Alice shot first. One, two, three, four times she drove the ball into the net. Then disaster struck. The fifth time, Matt dived full-length to tip the ball around the post. Super save!

Matt gave Alice the gloves. Then he scored with four low hard shots. That made him over-confident. He blasted his last kick even harder – and it sailed over the bar. Tie: four goals each.

"Someone's got to pay for another round!" said Jay.

Emma nodded. "Why not make it the best of three?"

"Make it fifteen," Matt snarled at Alice. "I'll still win."

"Yeah, right," Alice gazed skywards. "Oh look – low-flying pigs!"

"For heaven's sake!" Mr Pitt cut in. "Let's keep this competition *healthy*, shall we!"

And so it began. Amazingly, the contest did go to the best of fifteen rounds. Then twenty-five. Then *thirty*-five!

People couldn't rush up fast enough to clink their coins into Mr Pitt's box. But still there was no winner. Each time Matt scored five, Alice hit five too. And if either of them missed, they made sure they then saved one to even up the scores.

They both wanted to win so badly. Needed to. But as Jay kept a count of all the money flowing in, he saw a way for *everyone* to be a winner that day. When Matt and Alice swapped gloves again, he whispered a few words to them. At first Matt and Alice both looked shocked, then they looked at each other thoughtfully.

"Go get more punters!" yelled Jay, turning to his classmates. "Tell 'em *this* is where it's at!"

While they sped away, Jay smiled across at the Head and then winked.

Twenty minutes later dozens of new people turned up.

Most were glad to quit the World Cup game, which had turned into a total yawn. The rest left the street party when the barbecue caught fire. Even a local newspaper reporter tagged along, after being deafened at the pop concert.

By now Mr Pitt was taking money for a Best of 65! The Head was really pleased. She'd worked out what Jay had told Matt and Alice to do. By keeping this contest on the boil, they kept the money flowing in – edging them ever closer to the fête's £2000 target. But still they both *pretended* to be mad keen to win each round. So the frantic punters kept paying up – taking the shoot-out to the Best of 75, 85, 95!

Then with the score at Matt 40 wins, Alice 40 wins and 15 tied rounds, Jay gave a thumbs-up signal to the Head, who stepped in with a grin and called a halt.

"I declare Matt and Alice joint winners," she said. "But more importantly, Jay has worked out that we now have enough money to start work on the school pool."

A massive cheer went up. "But who's the FTF?" Emma shouted.

"Me!" whooped Mr Pitt, jamming the cardboard crown on his own head and dancing away. "*I'm* the Fête's Top Fundraiser!"

"Sorry, Mr Pitt," the Head called after him. "But I think the title goes to Jay!"

Jay shook his head at his teacher. "Some people are *so* competitive," he said with a sad smile. "It never crosses their minds to co-operate."

School Fête Shoot-out!

Amazing Saturday Afternoon Showdown!

Alice Foster shoots against Matt Henderson

At Fleetwood Primary's fête, pupils Alice Foster and Matthew Henderson took part in an incredible penalty shoot-out arranged by their classmate Jay Oakes. Between them they took 950 spot-kicks – and still neither of them could be declared the outright winner! With spectators paying 40p per kick, however, the pupils raised a fantastic £380. Added to the rest of the fête's funds, this was enough to start restoring the old school swimming pool.